W9-AVJ-652

Henry Holt and Company, LLC
Publishers since 1866
175 Fifth Avenue
New York, New York 10010
www.HenryHoltKids.com

Henry Holt® is a registered trademark
of Henry Holt and Company, LLC.

Library of Congress Cataloging-in-Publication Data
Martin, Bill
White Dynamite and Curly Kidd.
Summary: Lucky Kidd watches her father ride a mean bull at
the rodeo and thinks about becoming a bull rider herself.
[1. Rodeos—Fiction. 2. Fathers and daughters—Fiction.]
I. Archambault, John. II. Rand, Ted, ill. III. Title.
PZ7.M356773Wh 1986 [E] 85-27214

ISBN-13: 978-0-8050-1018-3 / ISBN-10: 0-8050-1018-1
15 14 13 12 11

First published in hardcover in 1986 by Henry Holt and Company
First paperback edition, 1989
Printed in China on acid-free paper. ∞

White Dynamite & Curly Kidd

By Bill Martin Jr. & John Archambault

Illustrated by Ted Rand

Henry Holt and Company / New York

It's about time, Dad.
   Yep.
Are ya' scared?
   Nope.
I am.
   Don't need to be.
I just can't help it.
   Guess not.
Why don't ya' get scared, Dad?
   I think.
About what?
   About places.
What kind of places?
   Places I'd like to go.
   Places I'd like to see.
I'd like to go ta' Riverton
to see Grandma.
   She'd like that.

Here comes Dynamite, Dad.
   Yep.
They're puttin' him in the chute.
   Yep.
He sure looks mean.
   He's mean all right.
But a mean bull means extra points.
   Yep.
So you were lucky to get him, huh?
   Yep, luck of the draw.
They say he's the meanest bull
in the whole United States.
   Yep.
But you're the best bull rider
in the whole United States
. . . and Canada, huh?
   Could be.

He sure looks mean, Dad.
　Yep.
Maybe he's just actin' mean.
　Nope, he ain't actin'.
　He's natural mean.
Double-rank mean, huh?
　Yep.
Maybe I'll be a bull rider
when I grow up.
　Could be.
Would you like that, Dad?
Me bein' a bull rider?
　Sure, why not?

I'd want ever'body to know
that Curly Kidd's my dad.
   Me too.
So I'll be Number 13, too
just like you.
   13–2.
   Good number.
And my rodeo name'll be
Curly Kidd's Little Kid.
Do you like that, Dad?
   Nope.
Then I'll just use my plain ol' name,
Lucky Kidd.
   Sounds good to me.

Ya' want a stick of gum, Dad?
   Thanks.
You can have two if ya' want.
   Thanks.
I always chew two, too.
Keeps me calm.
   Me too.
Do you want another stick?
You can have three if ya' want.
   Nope . . . two'll do.

The bull's in, Dad.
Here goes.
    Yep.
Are you all set?
Rope tight?
    Yep.
Good luck, Dad.
Have a safe trip.
    Yep.

Oh, I'm so scared.
I gotta think hard about places . . .
to keep me calm . . .
     Riverton Wyoming . . .
        maybe Casper
        an' Cheyenne
Another place
I wanta go
   . . . someday . . . is

Oh!
He's outa the chute!
Gone plumb dumb wild!
    KAN-*sas*
    TEX-*as*
    U-*tah*
    MAINE

That bull's pitchin'
with all his might . . .
twenty-four tons
a' White Dynamite!

Stick with 'im, Dad!
AL-*a*-BAM-*a*
MINN-*e*-SOT-*a*
IN-*di*-AN-*a*
AR-*i*-ZO-na

Leapin' like a bull frog . . .
   O-*ma*-HA *ne*-BRAS-*ka*
Dustin' up the Big Sky . . .
   KET-*chi*-KAN *a*-LAS-*ka*
Landin' hard . . .
   new MEX-*i*-CO

Four seconds down, Dad!
Four more to go!

Oh! Dad's in the rocker now . . .
floppin' back and forth!
His head's goin' south!
Bull's goin' north . . .
An' I'm goin' ta'
        WEST *vir*-GIN-*ia*
        PLAIN *vir*-GIN-*ia*
        CAL-*gar*-Y *stam*-PEDE!

Oh, that bull's twistin' . . .
twistin' like a corkscrew
straight down the right-a-way.
His middle name's Doomsday!
  U! S! A!

You're winnin', Dad!
You're winnin'!

Rackin'!
Crackin'!
The bull's sky trackin' . . .
tiltin' to the right
in a belly roll . . . .

Say hey Willie May!
Ya' lucked out, Dad
with your left-hand hold!
     ver-MONT!

. . . Oh, my gosh!
There goes my gum!

He's hookin' right!
Now hookin' left!
Only one second left, Dad!
Keep him covered.
Stick to him like glue!

Yah! Hoo!
    KAL-*ama*-ZOO
Tic! Tac! Toe!
    I-*da*-HO

You did it, Dad!

RIV-*er*-TON
an' WAL-*la*-WAL-*la* WASH-*ing*-TON!

Hey, Dad!
You did it!
You won, Dad!
You won!
You prouded me, Dad.
You sure prouded me.
You rode him like glue!

You hear that, Dad?
97 points!
97 out of a hun'erd!
I guess that makes you
the best bull rider
in all the United States!
—*and* Canada!
—*and* Mexico!
   97 ain't perfect.
In my book it is.
You're perfect, Dad!
Total!
All together,
top to bottom,
inside out,
and outside in,
my dad is total perfect!
   That's a lotta words, Lucky.
Hey, Dad!
You're limpin'!
   Am I?

Are ya hurt?
    Don't know.
Don't know?
You oughta know.
It's your foot!
    Can't tell.
How come?
    My head's still ridin' that bull.
Well, my heart's still ridin' too, Dad.
It's takin' an awful poundin'.
    Well, ya' better get used to it, Lucky . . .

. . . if you're gonna be a bull rider.